Richard Scarry's
BIG
and
LITTLE

A BOOK OF OPPOSITES

A GOLDEN BOOK • NEW YORK
Western Publishing Company, Inc., Racine, Wisconsin 53404

ISBN 0-307-11928-9/ISBN 0-307-61928-1 (lib. bdg.)   B C D E F G H I J

Kitty has a great, big doll.
Flossie has a little doll.

big

little

Henny is big and her children are little.

big

little

little

big

Squeaky Mouse is little and Bully Bobcat is big.

big **little**

Bilgy is blowing bubbles.
Some are big and some are little.

Hilda is big...

big

...and Squeaky is little.

little

tall

tall

short

Tom Cat has built a very tall tower of blocks. The tower is almost as tall as the giraffe. Babykins looks very short next to the giraffe and the tower.

GoGo is cutting the tall grass. Now poor Gus will have to find somewhere else to hide. The grass is too short.

short

tall

long

Chips Beaver is sawing a long board in half. Then he will have two short boards.

short

Noah, the long boa constrictor, loves to eat bananas. Squigley is short next to Noah.

short

long

Big Hilda can't get into the room
because the door is too narrow.
"You need a wide door," says Squeaky.

The street is wide, and Ali Cat is painting
a narrow line on the street.

Farmer HeeHaw has apple trees growing on the hill. One tree trunk is thick, and one is thin. The vegetables growing in the vegetable patch look short growing beside the tall corn.

thick

thin

tall

short

straight

curved

The barn has a wide door and a narrow door.
The wide path coming from the wide door is straight.
The narrow path coming from the narrow door is curved.

Mr. Fixit Fox and Chips are sawing branches. Mr. Fixit Fox is sawing a thin branch. Chips is sawing a thick branch. What will happen?

thin

thick

Jack Sprat could eat no fat,
His wife could eat no lean,
And so between them both, you see,
They licked the platter clean.

thin

fat

Pickles Pig eats too much pie,
and that is why he is so fat.

fat

Squigley can crawl through a hollow log
because he is very thin.

thin

tight   loose

Pickles Pig's clothes are
too tight. Wiggles's clothes
are too loose. Do you
think their mothers bought
the wrong size?

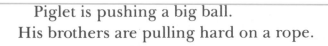

Piglet is pushing a big ball.
His brothers are pulling hard on a rope.

push

pull

hide

seek

Wiggles and Hooligan are playing
hide-and-seek.

Froggie likes to play leapfrog.
Run and jump. Jump over a frog.

over

under

top

up

down

bottom

out

in

Huckle and Nicky go
up and down, up and down
on the see-saw.

Brother Bear has climbed
to the top of the jungle gym.
Kitty is still at the bottom.

Baby Pig is sitting in the sandbox.
Babykins is playing out of the sandbox.

upstairs

downstairs

Wee Willie Winkie runs through the town,
Upstairs and downstairs, in his nightgown;
Rapping at the window, crying through the lock,
Are the children all in bed, for now it's eight o'clock?

Jack, be nimble,
Jack, be quick,
Jack, jump over
The candlestick.

over

Where is the little boy
Tending the sheep?
He's under the haycock,
Fast asleep.

under

Here are some things we do each day.

asleep

awake

stand

sit

in

out

talk

listen

up

down

Daddy wants the piglets to go. The piglets don't want to go.
Daddy is making sure that they go. Where?

sad

Of course! It's bathtime. The piglets don't like
water and soap. Just look at all those tears. They are so sad.

The piglets are playing at the beach.
What fun to bury Daddy and build a castle on
his tummy. Now the piglets are happy.

happy

clean   **dirty**

Flossie's ears are clean.
Wiggles's ears are dirty.

Flossie is quite disgusted
with Wiggles. He is messy,
and she is neat.

neat   **messy**

good

bad

The children are going into class
quietly. They are being good.

Oh, dear! The naughty boys are
fighting. They are being bad.

Kitty is sharing her dolls.
She is a polite kitten.

polite

rude

Bully is kicking
Babykins's sand castle.
He is being very rude.

open

closed

Big Hilda is yawning. Her mouth is wide open.
Cover your mouth, Hilda. Don't be rude.

Flossie's kite is high in the sky.
Hooligan's kite is flying very low.

Wiggles is jumping
over the fence. Nicky is
crawling under the fenc

over

unde

on

Ali Cat is walking
on the fence.
Squeaky is falling off
the fence.

off

up

down

top

Kitty is standing at the bottom
of the ladder. Tom is standing
on the top...for now.

bottom

full   empty

in   out

Spud Bugs is going in the hollow log.
Squigley is crawling out the other end.

summer

winter

In the summer it is hot.

In the winter it is cold.

hot

Hey, Whiff, your truck is on fire! Don't you feel how hot it is?

cold

Pickles Pig opened the cold refrigerator so often that he caught a cold.

In the daytime, it is light.
At night, it is dark.

Turkle Turtle is getting wet,
but he is keeping the chicks dry.

Wiggles wears his raincoat to wash the dishes.

above

behind

back

middle

below

The driver is at the front of the bus.
Haggis is reading his newspaper at the back.
Dingo is driving his sports car ahead of the bus.
Wiggles is riding his unicycle behind.
The bee is flying above the bus.
What is below the bus? Who is sitting in the middle of the bus?

front

ahead

Sneakers is showing you left and right.
He put a sneaker on his left foot.
His right foot is bare.

left ← → right

left   right

Bumbles is writing on the board.
He writes from left to right.

Ali Cat is drawing a straight line.
Do you know in which direction
he is moving?
Did you say to the right?
Good for you!

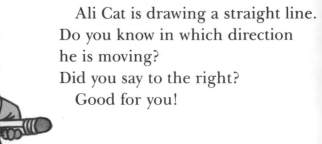